C000119941

TWELVE DAYS OF CHRISTMAS HORROR VOLUME 3

RICK WOOD

BLOOD SPLATTER PRESS

RICK WOOD

Rick Wood is a British writer born in Cheltenham.

His love for writing came at an early age, as did his battle with mental health. After defeating his demons, he grew up and became a stand-up comedian, then a drama and English teacher, before giving it all up to become a full-time author.

He now lives in Loughborough, where he divides his time between watching horror, reading horror, and writing horror.

ALSO BY RICK WOOD

The Sensitives
The Sensitives
My Exorcism Killed Me
Close to Death
Demon's Daughter
Questions for the Devil
Repent
The Resurgence
Until the End

Blood Splatter Books
Psycho B*tches
Shutter House
This Book is Full of Bodies
Home Invasion
Haunted House
Woman Scorned

Non-Fiction
How to Write an Awesome Novel
The Writer's Room

Rick also publishes thrillers under the pseudonym Ed Grace...
Jay Sullivan
Assassin Down
Kill Them Quickly
The Bars That Hold Me
A Deadly Weapon

SANTA VS KRAMPUS
PART ONE

The blizzard rages across the North Pole, balls of white dancing across the wind.

The howls of the storm combine into a symphony of terror, a sound almost as furious as the sight. Animals hide in shelters that the elements plot to destroy, their fur coats not enough to stop them shivering.

The crunch of his footstep barely makes a sound in the wrath of the storm. But, when he witnesses the sight before him, Santa Claus no longer thinks about the tempest that freezes his bones.

"Who did this..."

Spots of blood create a path to the elves' quarters, growing larger as he proceeds toward a mat that reads *All Friends Welcome Here.*

He pauses. He has a duty of care to the elves; he wants to know what has happened. But he can't be reckless. Barging in won't help anyone, so he proceeds with caution, one step at a time; his large, black, leather boots sinking into the thick snow as he approaches.

No sounds come from the within the cabin; not that he'd hear anything in this storm. The wind would disguise any scream that would otherwise have echoed into the night. Even so, he listens as he peers through the window. The glass is covered in frost and mist, concealing any figures that lie within; only revealing the flickering amber of the candles inside.

He places his gloved hand onto the handle. Stiffens his muscles. Flexes his fingers. Opens the door.

It creaks into the darkness.

He steps inside. He pulls the light switch, but it doesn't work. That must be why the elves lit the candles.

He takes a few more careful steps forward, looking from one bed to the other, each half the size of his.

They are empty.

The spots of blood continue across the wooden floorboards. What starts out as splodges turns into a large streak, like someone has been dragged.

A few more steps and he hears breaths. Murmurs of fear.

"Santa..."

The whisper distracts him. He looks to the corner of the room and finally sees the elves. They cling together. All ten of them who share this room, shaking, gripped by fear.

No, wait.

There isn't ten of them. Only eight.

"Where's Flopsy and Popsy?" he asks.

They dare not reply. The elf at the front, Joppy – the bravest one, if one can ever say that an elf is brave – raises a quivering arm and points at the door to the bathroom.

Santa takes a candle and approaches. He almost slips on the blood, but manages to steady himself.

He places a hand against the door and pushes it. It opens a crack, then resists. Something is blocking it from opening. With more force, Santa barges open the door, and Popsy's wide, still eyes stare up at him.

At first, Santa doesn't understand. Why is Popsy lying there? And why is Popsy just staring at him?

He sees the blood across Popsy's throat, but it doesn't register, not at first. He sees the large bite mark that exposes Popsy's windpipe; he sees missing teeth in a jaw bent to the side; he sees the slit down Popsy's chest that reveals his still heart, half the literal size of a human's, but figuratively bigger than anyone's; and he realises...

"Fuck... Popsy... You're dead..."

There is a noise coming from the shadows. Like a sucking noise. Someone eating or drinking something, slurping and slopping and splishing and–

A face glistens in a small gift of light.

"No!"

Flopsy lies across its lap, his head hanging off his body like a ball on a string. His eyes don't stare at Santa because they are not there. One eyeball is missing, the other is hanging out of the mouth of the creature. Flopsy's belly is slit open and most of his insides gone, devoured by this beast; the creature that Santa struggles to make out in the darkness.

"Let him go," Santa's voice booms out.

The creature stops. Santa can't see its face, but he feels the grin that spreads across it. It slowly lifts its visage, revealing itself in the soft glow of Santa's candle, and Santa recoils in horror at the sight of his mortal enemy.

"You!"

It wears a tatty red coat with padded trimming, as if to mock him. Beneath its hood is a face as devilish as a face can be. Two horns curve toward the roof; a long, red tongue flaps from between its fangs; its tail thrashes back and forth as if excited; its nose and eyes, though technically human-like, are nothing of the sort, with blood-red pupils and red snot dripping from the nostrils; and its body, covered in fur, has two arms that end in claws, with long, spindly, bony fingers, and long, brown and sharp nails.

Krampus.

Santa's mortal enemy.

"How dare you..."

It cackles. How silly you are, Santa, to think that your command of *let him go* would quell the beast. It feeds off Santa's horror, energises itself from it, soaks it in. There is nothing in Santa's immediate anger that could do anything but provide more satisfaction to the terror the monster has created.

"Put. Flopsy. Down."

The command goes unheeded. Santa steps forward, the violence of Flopsy's death growing in clarity as his candle graces the body with more light.

"I said put him down."

Krampus drops the elf, but only so it can stand and stretch its body upwards, its hooves scraping the roof, towering over Santa, placing the figure of Christmas in the shadow of evil.

"You leave the elves alone – this is between *you* and *me*."

Krampus roars then laughs, the moisture of its rancid breath creating a warmth; flickers of putrid saliva landing on Santa's face.

"Listen to me, you fucker. Enough is enough. Tonight, we end this – once and for all."

Santa steps toward Krampus, which is supposed to be an intimidating gesture, but only shows how much greater in size Krampus is.

"I'm going to show you just what Santa Claus is about."

Krampus laughs once again, followed by a mocking sneer, then swipes its claws at Santa's head and launches him at the far wall of the bathroom. The wooden beams separating the elves from the elements collapse as Santa's body flies through them, and he lands in the middle of the storm.

He rolls to his side, submerged in snow, rubbing his head.

Krampus leaps from the elves' quarters, soaring through the blizzard, and its legs land either side of Santa.

He knows this is going to be a long, long night, but he doesn't care – the battle to end all battles has finally begun.

Santa Vs Krampus continues later in the anthology.

CHARADES WITH A SIDE OF RAGE

The flashing blue lights of static police cars illuminate the street. Nosy neighbours, interrupted from their Christmas evening festivities, twitch their curtains, put on a dressing gown, and make their way outside, both disgruntled by the intrusion and morbidly curious by the scene. They are kept back from the house by police tape and two officers standing sternly with their arms behind their backs.

The house itself is a grand, pristine cottage in the Cotswolds. The white picket fence surrounds a well-cut lawn and budding flowers. On the driveway sits a BMW, sparkling in the streetlight. The house is painted immaculately, expensive garden ornaments decorate the path – and the inside of the living room window is covered in streams of blood.

Whispers and murmurs pass through the neighbours, facts turning to non-facts like a game of Chinese whispers. What starts as a comment about someone being hurt passes through multiple voyeurs, and ends up as an assertion that a mad serial killer has eaten the entire family.

One woman – the neighbourhood know-it-all who tries to sound posher than she is – approaches a police officer and asks, "Whatever is going on?"

"We can't say anything at this time, Ma'am."

But the police officer doesn't need to say anything. The front door opens and multiple gurneys wheel body bags over the garden path, past the garden gnomes and cat repellent.

"But – but they were so nice," the know-it-all says. "How could this happen to them? Did someone attack them?"

The police officer looks over his shoulder, checks the coast is clear, then says, under his breath, "There is no sign that anyone else was ever there."

"You mean, they did this to themselves?"

He raises his eyebrows and resumes his cold resolve.

"Why, whatever could have driven them to this..."

Six Hours Earlier...

"Why, that was exquisite!" declares Reginald. "Absolutely exquisite! The best feast we've ever had!"

"It truly was," replies Angela, and their children, Edgar and Jessabelle, nod in eager agreement.

"Oh, chef!" she calls out.

A woman wearing a smart white blouse, black trousers and an apron enters.

"That was wonderful – please do tell the rest of the staff."

"Thank you, Ma'am," the woman says, nodding timidly. "We are all packed up now. Unless you need anything else?"

"No, please, do go, enjoy the rest of your Christmas."

The woman nods and, after a few minutes, the noises in the kitchen end and the staff have left.

"Well, shall we retire to the living room?" asks Reginald. "Have some brandy?"

"That sounds wonderful."

And so there they are, ten minutes later, sat in the living room, their bellies bursting. Once they are settled, Reginald stands, raises his brandy glass, and declares, "I propose a toast!"

The children sit forward and clap their hands together.

"Oh, yay!"

"Oh, I do love Daddy's toasts!"

"To my wonderful family," Reginald says. "My wife, Angela, who has shown endless caring for our children. Honestly, the lengths you went to in order to find the right nanny were nothing short of heroic. Well done to you."

"Oh, please Reginald, you're going to make me blush."

"And those camellias outside – you chose the perfect gardener. You really are quite proud of those camellias, aren't you?"

"Yes, I am." She beams.

"And to my children – Edgar, the captain of the debate team, and soon to be head boy of Eaton Boy's Senior. Honestly, the things you do for that school – where would they be without you?"

"Thank you, Daddy, you are too kind."

"And Jessabelle – soon to join the Eaton Girl's Senior. What can I say? Captain of the football team, netball team, and consistently an A star student. I am ever so proud of you, darling."

"Oh, thank you, Daddy, really, it's nothing."

"And so I raise a glass and propose a toast – to us. May nothing ever get in our way."

The children raise their glasses of milk, Angela raises her brandy, and together, they repeat, "To us!"

They all take a sip of their drinks, and a moment of comfortable silence follows.

"So, what shall we do now?" Angela asks.

"Oh, I know!" offers Edgar. "Why don't we play a game? A game of, say... charades?"

"Oh, what a droll idea!" Jessabelle declares.

"Oh, yes, very droll indeed – who would like to go first?"

Edgar raises his arm.

"Ah, of course, the reigning charades champion. Please, if you will."

Edgar stands, places his milk on a coaster, then thinks for a moment. He always thinks of the best ones, so his family are happy to give him a moment. After a few seconds, he grins – he has a brilliant one. He makes the motion of a camera.

"Film," they all observe.

He lifts four fingers.

"Four words," they concur.

He lifts one finger.

"First word."

He puts his hand over his eyes like he's searching for something, then pretends to act puzzled when he can't find it.

"Lost!"

"Searching!"

"Somewhere!"

"Gone!"

He points at Jessabelle, who confirms that the word is *gone.*

Edgar lifts four fingers.

"Fourth word!"

He wafts a hand behind his bottom.

"Wind!"

He nods, and Angela confirms, "Gone with the Wind!"

Edgar cheers and they all clap.

All except Reginald.

"I don't think that was very amusing," he mutters.

"What's that, dear?" Angela asks.

"Pretending to pass wind. It's rude."

"It's just a bit of fun."

"Yes, but there is no need to be rude."

Noticing her husband's displeasure, Angela quickly says, "Shall I go next?"

She stands, determined to remove the grimace from her husband's face.

She signals a film, and they confirm that it is a film, just as they confirm that it is two words. She then places two fingers either side of her breasts and pretends to be a t-rex.

"Jurassic Park!" the children cry out.

"Yes!"

"Well, that was a bit silly," Reginald says.

"What's that, dear?"

"You made yourself look like a bit of a wally."

"It's all in good fun, dear."

"Yes, we can have fun, but no need to make a show of yourself."

She smiles hesitantly. "Why don't you have a go, dear?"

"Okay then."

He stands. Signals a film. Then signals one word.

He lays on the floor and pretends to drown.

"Jaws!"

"Deep Blue Sea!"

"The Perfect Storm!"

"No!" he grumbles, and again pretends to drown, this time a bit more aggressively.

"Captain Phillips!"

"The Abyss!"

"I said it only had one word!" he snaps.

He pauses. Calms himself down. Reminds himself this is supposed to be fun. And he pretends to drown again.

There is silence as the family watches him. Then Angela cries out, "Pirates of the Caribbean!"

"I said one word! One word! *One bloody word!*"

"Okay, dear, no need to get angry – I'm sure we'll get it."

Once again, he lays on the floor, bashes his arms around like he's drowning, and his family stare at him expectantly.

Silence lingers through the room.

He thrashes his arms more fervently.

The silence gets awkward.

Then, deciding to break the tension, Angela says, "Are you sure it's not Pirates of the Caribbean?"

Reginald stands and throws his late father's clock from the fireplace to the floor.

"No! I think I would know if it was Pirates of the ruddy Caribbean! I am the one doing it after all!"

He lays down on the floor and pretends to drown again, staring at his wife with a demented, determined, furious expression.

"But I really think it's Pirates of the–"

"It was Titanic!" he bellows, standing over her. "Titanic! *Titanic! Tifuckingtanic!*"

His face is red. He's panting. His fists clench.

"Okay dear, no need to get angry."

"Get angry? I said it was one word and you repeatedly

say it's something that has *four bloody words*! Are you a *damn imbecile!*"

Angela stands. "No need to get rude!"

"Then stop being such a fool!"

The children gasp. Their father never usually calls their mother such a word.

"Me? A fool? How dare you!"

"Yes. And you know what? That nanny you picked – she's not that great."

The children gasp again. Angela's eyes widen until they look like they are about to burst out of their sockets.

"You take that back!" she demands.

"No. And you know what else?" He moves his face to within inches of hers. "The camellias in the garden look like they were pulled out of my arse."

She slaps him instinctively. The children gasp again.

"What are you gasping about?" Angela snaps. "Your wind mime was inappropriate; this is all your fault!"

"It's not his fault," Jessabelle objects.

"Hey," interjects Edgar. "I can stand up for myself!"

"You just slapped me!" Reginald screams, returning the focus to what really matters. "Stop telling them off, you just slapped me!"

He slaps her back.

She stands back, aghast. She picks the clock Reginald threw across the room from the chair and smacks him around the head with it.

He gasps. He searches the room. He rips the 68-inch HD plasma television out of the wall and brings it down on her head.

She immediately stands, lifting the television and hurtling it back.

He trips her up, lifts the end of the luxury leather

Chesterfield Sofa, and drops it on her head, which squelches under the impact.

"Oh my gosh!" Edgar cries. "You killed my mother!"

Reginald's eyes turn to his children. Bloodshot. Glaring. Intense.

"Don't. You. Talk. To. Me. Like. That."

He rips the John Richard Brutalist table lamp from the wall and approaches his two cowering prides of joy.

Christmas Night

With her arms crossed and her head shaking, the know-it-all stares at the bodies being loaded into the back of the ambulance.

"Oh my," she says. "Whatever could have driven such a lovely family to such a fate?"

Her nosy neighbour friends nod in agreement as they shed a customary tear or two.

Then the door to her own home opens, and a smart, well-spoken child stands on the porch and calls to her.

"Mother!" the child says. "We're waiting for you!"

"I'll be a minute darling."

"But Gilbert wishes to play charades, and we can't start without you!"

Her face brightens. "Oh, how lovely," she says, and hurries back inside.

She locks the door behind her.

DEFUNCT DECORATIONS

Dear Christmas Decorations Direct,

I must say, I am appalled with your service this year.

Every December 1st for the past fifteen years, I have come to you with my decorative needs, and each year you have supplied me with my exact requirements. I have had a sufficiently lovely Christmas as a result, and have never been let down.

Until this year.

My misery on this Christmas Eve was caused entirely by your decorations. I am thoroughly disappointed, and will be hesitant to use your service again next year.

And what exactly is it I have found disappointing with your decorations?

Well, where do I even start?

Take your tinsel, for example.

Last year, it had the strength of rope, and the yield of metal. I could wrap it around a young woman's throat, and it would not so much as wince under the strain of her struggling windpipe.

This year, however, I wrapped the tinsel around the throat of a young Vietnamese prostitute I picked up on Dowry Street, and it took a mere eight seconds until it snapped.

The woman almost got away!

You can just imagine the furore that occurred as a result. I had to chase her throughout my abode, and she almost made it into the garden.

I thought it was me – that my strength was the problem. I am a year older than I was last Christmas, after all.

So I tried again.

I wrapped the tinsel around her throat – thrice, this time, inside of the standard double wrapping I normally use.

And what happened?

The damn thing snapped again!

I mean, what is the point of me going to you with my decorative needs if you do not supply me with tinsel that has sufficient yield? It's almost like you don't want me to murder escorts!

In the end, I had to smack her head repeatedly against the fireplace until her body stopped throbbing, which was most disappointing. I hoped to asphyxiate her so her face would still be intact. After impaling her repeatedly against a solid surface, she looked hideous. I could barely maintain my erection as I made love to her corpse.

And the baubles. Normally, they are sufficiently big that they will choke a person when stuffed down their throat, but still small enough that they will fit in the first place.

But, no!

No matter how much I rammed and rammed, shoved and shoved, poked and prodded, the bauble would not go further than the back of her mouth. I mean, how am I supposed to choke my grandma if the bauble won't fit down her wrinkly neck?

And don't even get me started on the chocolate treats I acquired from you. I gave them to the local children who came carolling at my door, and the poison inside the treats didn't even knock them out! I heard from their parents that they were sick, but that is all.

How am I supposed to deal with carollers if there is not a sufficient quantity of poison in the chocolate?

And the model nativity scene you sent me was just ridiculous. It was not realistic in the slightest. I mean, Mary was sat there holding a baby in her arms, looking happy and beautiful. She'd just given birth for Christ's sake! She should be bloated, red-faced, possibly even dead considering she was giving birth 2000 years ago at a time when there were no trained mid-wives.

And yet you give me a scene of contentedness to show the realistic nature of our messiah's birth?

What kind of sick individual designed that?

Similarly, the wreath you sent to me. It hangs on the door perfectly, making it look festive. But have you tried putting it around a person's neck?

It was so loose I could fit my hand in with my wife's throat! She thought I put it on her as a joke. She even laughed. And now she's still alive, and I'm having to visit my mother-in-law for Christmas lunch.

My mother-in-law, dear retailer.

DO YOU KNOW WHAT YOU HAVE DONE?

And, speaking of which, those glass ornaments you gave me...

I smashed them, and the shards were barely enough to cut my own leg. How am I supposed to use them on my mother-in-law when they barely draw blood?

I hope that you take this letter in the spirit in which it is meant – both a rant, and constructive criticism. Should you address my needs and rectify these issues, I will consider purchasing from you again next year. Until then, you can expect me to be providing another Christmas decoration company with my custom.

As an apology, I would be willing to accept store discount.

Yours sincerely,

A very annoyed person.

SANTA VS KRAMPUS
PART TWO

Santa is too old for this shit.

That's what comes with being immortal – you age more and more, and the aches grow stronger and stronger, and it never ends. Maybe it wouldn't be too bad if Krampus put him out of his misery. Maybe it would be an act of mercy on the part of his mortal enemy.

Or maybe it would destroy the hopes and dreams of millions of children across the world.

His head rolls on its side. His neck muscles prick. He sees beyond the elves' quarters, to the barn where his sleigh and reindeer are kept. Then he sees Mrs Claus.

What the hell is Martha doing here?

She walks out from behind the barn, a tray of cookies in her hands. Despite the rabid storm, he swears he can smell cinnamon. His favourite.

Krampus's face lowers toward Santa's. Its grin widens. Its laugh is low and menacing. Its taunt unmistakable.

It traces its claw up Santa's fat belly, up his chest, and to his throat, wanting to make it nice and slow.

Then it realises that Santa is distracted by something over its shoulder.

Krampus turns its head and sees her.

Santa's chest seizes with terror.

"No!" Santa cries. Not her. Never her.

He grabs hold of the rags around Krampus's chest, uses them to pull himself up, then swipes an elbow into his enemy's jaw. It has little to no effect, it just amuses the beast; but it allows Santa a moment to scamper away, despite the thick snow slowing his run to a quick walk.

Martha sees him and smiles. She has cookies for him. It's the night before Christmas Eve, and she knows this is when he gets most anxious, just as she knows a tray of cookies helps to calm him.

Then she sees it. And she drops the cookies. And she screams.

"Martha, run!" Santa cries, but it's too late. Krampus leaps toward her, using its hooves and claws to project himself through the air.

Santa runs after it. At least, he tries. As she runs away, her figure becomes barely discernible amongst the frantic snowflakes flying in all different directions, and she disappears in the storm.

But he can make out Krampus's silhouette. That is unmistakable. It is heading toward the barn.

That is where Martha must have gone.

Santa tries harder to sprint, but he can barely walk. The snow is up to his knees. He has to pull his leg out with every step, and it takes too long.

Krampus's outline lands on the roof of the barn. If he kills the reindeer, there's no more Christmas. But if he kills Martha, then there's no more Santa.

All he can do is move forward at a frantically slow pace. Lifting one leg up, then the other.

The sound of Krampus tearing at pieces of the barn roof grows louder beneath the screeches of wind.

As Santa gains on the barn, he can see Krampus

digging its claws into the wood, grabbing planks and throwing them away, trying to find its way in. Trying to torment Santa with the violent death of his beloved before his own demise.

Not today, Krampus.

Not today.

Santa eventually reaches the barn and, unseen by Krampus – who is too distracted with creating a hole in the roof big enough for him to fit through – unlocks the door Martha would have locked behind her.

He throws himself inside and looks around. The reindeer are awake and alert. Pieces of wood fall onto the sleigh that sits proudly in the middle of the floor.

"Martha?"

Her head lifts from behind Prancer and Dancer. He rushes over to her, limping slightly, and throws his arms around her. He holds her close. She smells sweet, just as she always does. He met her in a bakery, just over 140 years ago. Their love has never wavered since. His heart still warms at the sight of her rosy cheeks and cheeky smile. Having been alive since 240 A.D., he'd left his birthplace of Myra – what is now known as Turkey – and searched the world for meaning to his lengthened existence. He was the patron saint of children. In his youth, he'd saved three girls from going into slavery by providing them with a dowry so they could marry, and the action had not gone unnoticed.

There was widespread anguish when the Dutch reported on his apparent death in 1773. But they were mistaken. Even so, it gave him a quieter life for a while.

But none of it meant anything until he met her.

She was the one who showed him that he could deliver all those toys in one night. She was the one who showed him how magic the North Pole could truly be. It was her who was truly the heart and soul of Christmas – not him.

It was all her.

And he would do anything to protect her.

The roof above rips apart. Krampus is almost in.

"Hide," Santa tells her, then rushes to Prancer and Dancer, and attaches their reins to his sleigh. He doesn't have time to attach all the reindeer, so he won't be able to fly too high off the ground, but he'll at least be able to draw the monster away from everything he holds dear.

"What are you doing?" she cries.

"I'm leading it away."

The roof rips open. Krampus's shadow overtakes the barn.

"But he'll kill you."

He looks back at her. She looks distraught. She looks terrified. And she looks beautiful.

"I love you," he tells her, then turns away. She shouts something, but he doesn't hear what it is.

Krampus drops through the hole he created and shakes the ground with the impact of his hooves.

"Come on then, you little prick."

Santa flicks the reins, his wife opens the barn doors, and his two faithful reindeers charge into the storm. The snow slows them down for a few seconds, then they rise above it, flying just metres above the ground. This is as high as they'll get, but it'll do.

He checks over his shoulder, fearing that Krampus had stayed to finish off Martha before giving chase; but Krampus doesn't want to lose him, and is galloping after him, using his claws and hooves to leap into the air, land, then leap again.

The sleigh moves quickly, but Krampus is moving just as quick. The monster isn't even sweating. Santa isn't even sure the creature can perspire. He isn't even sure what the creature is. There is no name for it. There are no others that Santa is aware of.

It is just one creature, created for a single, sole purpose: to destroy Christmas and everything it stands for.

In other words, to destroy Santa.

"Not today, you ugly bastard," Santa growls, and flicks the reins again, urging the reindeer to go quicker.

He knows that Krampus will keep up.

He knows that he can't run forever.

He knows that, eventually, he'll have to fight.

But, for the moment, all Santa cares about is luring Krampus away from his home, and toward the north pole.

And by that, Santa doesn't mean the place, the North Pole. They are already there. He means the pole which is at the most north point of Earth. The pole that sticks out of the ground, marking the North Pole.

The pole that Santa had left there, quite deliberately, just in case he needed it.

The pole with a sharpened tip, pointed enough to draw blood from any despicable creature.

Just a little further, that's all. Just a little further.

Krampus's cackles carry along the gusts of wind. It knows that Santa will have to stop, eventually. All Santa is doing is tiring himself out. Making himself an easier target.

He just has to get a little further...

There it is. He sees it. Long, with red and white stripes, like a massive candy cane.

He pulls on the reins and slows Prancer and Dancer

down. They pass the pole and, as they do, Santa dives out of the sleigh, rolls through the snow, and ends up on his knees in front of the weapon. He grabs it with both hands, pulls hard to remove it from the ground, and holds it high.

Krampus lands a few steps before him.

Santa always forgets how large Krampus is. How much it looms over him.

He twirls the pole. Licks his dry, cracked lips. Ignores the ache in his back.

"Come on then, you fucker."

Krampus launches itself forward and dives out of the way of Santa's first swing of the pole.

The pole is heavier than he remembers. Then again, everything is heavier these days. You don't get to be over 1,700 years old and not feel it in your muscles.

Santa readies the pole again, and Krampus charges at him, and he swings it, forcing Krampus to duck once more.

"Come on!"

Krampus charges forward again, and Santa swings the pole upwards, scraping along Krampus's chest with the point, even drawing a speck of blood.

He wants to pump his fist into the air, but he doesn't. It's a little scratch. Even so, it's the most damage he's ever done to it.

It doesn't charge at him again. Krampus just waits, narrowing its evil eyes, glaring intently.

Just as Santa begins to think *holy moly, I'm winning,* Krampus leaps across the air, lands its hoof on the arm that holds the pole, and snatches it away from him.

Santa cries out, but the pain is nothing compared to the devastation of losing his weapon. He tries reaching for it with his other hand, but Krampus lifts it out of his reach.

Krampus examines it closely, moving it across his vision.

All Santa can think is *I must get that back!*

That is when Krampus places it in his mouth and bites it in half, then bites it again, and again. He places the pieces on his tongue and swallows them, including the pointed end, gulping them down, ending his meal with a satisfying burp.

"No..."

Krampus takes its hoof off Santa's arm and kicks him across the snow.

Santa lands on his side. He groans. Rolls over.

He looks to his sleigh.

There are more weapons beneath it. Grenades, detonators, spears – everything he needs.

He just has to get to them, and hope that Krampus doesn't eat them either.

Santa Vs Krampus continues later in the anthology.

CAROLLING WITH KILLERS: THE SECOND YEAR

Hello, and welcome to my third Christmas anthology – what a delight it is to have you along for the ride!

You may recall that, in the previous volume, I had the wonderful opportunity to research the Christmas experience through the perspective of a few convicts. Through this research, I was able to go carolling with some truly marvellous characters.

Well, as luck would have it, they enjoyed my company so much that they invited me back again!

And oh, what merriment we had. It was lovely to see what the friends I made last year are up to now.

Bubba has made so much progress since last time I saw him. He even says that his murderous urges have decreased as a direct result of his joyous evening of carolling with me, and that he only thinks about chopping up his ex-wife with an axe 3 times a day now.

He has gone from 12 times a day to just 3! That's a 400% improvement! I am ever so proud of him.

And, of course, I was delighted to catch up with Johanna, whose misunderstanding last year with the prison officer she spilt boiling hot water over caused quite the raucous. There have been further misunderstandings where she has been accused of awful things.

They should really speak to her about it, instead of making assumptions, as she assured me quite confidently that she did not know who sharpened the end of her toothbrush, and she has no idea how it ended up in her hand whilst her visiting mother lay bleeding at her feet. The only possibility I can conceive of is that someone hurt her mother, placed the weapon in her hand, and ran off – in which case, it is so very terrible what they are saying about this poor young woman.

Bulldog is another fellow I met and was quite the character. He enjoyed showing me the new tattoos he'd acquired, and they were quite something. In fact, he has a new tattoo on the back of his shaved head. It's an old Hindu image that symbolises *peace*. Honestly, those people who are accusing him of being a Nazi are hugely mistaken.

On this year's carolling excursion, I had the opportunity to meet more lovely people who have had their image tarnished by the authorities in such an awful manner. Honestly, with so many of these convicts claiming they are innocent, they should really review how well the justice system is working.

There was Brian, who says that, whilst the semen found on the body they discovered in his attic was proven to be his, he has no idea how it got there.

Then there was Donny Corleone, who claims he's never been in the mafia, and that he has no idea what they are talking about, and that if anyone claims he was in the mafia again he'll put a hit out on them.

And then there was an ex-children's entertainer from the eighties, who I am not allowed to name for legal reasons, who claims that it was all just a big mistake, and he doesn't know where the footage came from.

And so, like last year, they introduced me to some new carols. I especially enjoyed the rendition of *Rudolph the*

Bat-Wielding Reindeer. No one will ever pick on his red nose again!

And so you can join me in the merriment of the occasion, I am sharing a few of the songs we performed to the various houses who were willing to open their doors to us, instead of turning out their lights and hiding behind their sofas.

God bless the season and, as my friends would say, tell anyone about these carols and you'll sleep with the fishes.

(Which I don't understand, as it can't be very easy to fall asleep in the ocean!)

Season's greetings.

Rudolph the Bat-Wielding Reindeer

Rudolph the bat-wielding reindeer
Is a story you've never been told,
'Cause when he swings it at you
You'd probably end up out cold,
All of the other reindeer
Used to shake and quiver in their knees,
He'd beat the crap out of them
And they'd lay on the floor, begging, "please..."

Then one foggy Christmas eve
Santa said "come to me,
Bats are so ineffective
Here, have a machete!"
And oh, how Rudolph loved it,
He even shouted out with glee,
"Watch out you other reindeers

You're all going to fear me!"

Now he's attacked the other reindeers
And chopped off their heads,
And if you ever saw them,
Well, you wouldn't, 'cause they're all dead!

Frosty the Hitman

Frosty the hitman
Was a cold and ruthless soul,
With a Glock 45 and a big hacksaw
And a heart made out of coal.

Frosty the hitman,
Costs 20 grand or so they said,
But for an extra ten he'd find your next of kin
And he'd mail them your head.

There must have been some cold, cold blood
In that three-piece suit he donned,
'Cause when they gave him a hit
That fucker was good as gone.

Frosty the hitman,
Is a scary bastard it's true,
You better hope on Christmas Day
That he doesn't come for you.

Walking in a Horror Wonderland

People scream, can you hear them?
On the snow blood is glistening,
A violent sight
We're scared tonight
Walking in a horror wonderland.

Hidden away is your Mommy,
So afraid of the zombie,
She says to keep dreaming
But you can't help screaming
As the undead eat all your brains.

In the haunted house we'll hear creaking,
We'll pretend it's just a mouse squeaking,
You will feel shaken
As your soul is taken
And feasted on by evil ghosts from hell.

Later on, they'll devour
All your innards while you cower,
To face petrified
The fact that you died
Being eaten in a horror wonderland

O Come All Ye Rageful

O come all ye rageful, hungry and craving
*   blood,*
O come ye, o come ye to eat some guts,

O come and eat it, squirming a man to eat.

O come let us eat his heart,
O come let us eat his liver,
O come let us eat his limbs,
The squirming man we caught.

FIVE CHRISTMAS
CRACKERS

5 CRACKERS TO GO

"And so will you be taking the dog for a walk?" Charlie's sister asked on the laptop screen.

"No, we're going to have dinner then have a nice evening in."

"How lovely. Well, I best let you get to it then. Happy Christmas!"

Charlie and his children, Sadie and Norman, all echoed "Happy Christmas" back, and Charlie ended the Skype call.

Almost as soon as he closed the laptop lid, Janet called out, "Dinner is ready!"

With a pleasure they couldn't contain, they rushed to the dining room and took their places around the table, excited for the grand meal the woman of the house had cooked. Janet always did the most wonderful Christmas dinners, and Charlie spent the whole year looking forward to it.

Even the dog, Milo, sat on his bed, waiting for his bit of Christmas turkey.

He thanked his wife as she placed a warm plate in front of him, then laid the table with various dishes and serving spoons. He helped himself to roasted carrots, steamed parsnips, stuffing, pigs in blankets, Yorkshire puddings, cabbage, and a bit of extra turkey.

But, just as Janet sat down and they began to lift their first bite of dinner to their mouths, Charlie remembered something.

"The crackers!"

They all put their forks down – of course, the crackers! How could they forget?

"And you are going to love the crackers I got this year," Charlie said as he walked over to the cupboard and pulled out a box. "I ordered them from this special place in Taiwan – they weren't cheap, either. In fact, it comes with a bit of a game."

"A game?" Janet echoed, and shared a playfully puzzled look with her children, who giggled.

"Indeed!"

He placed the box on the table and opened the lid.

"What's more, we have five crackers – the perfect amount."

"But there's only four of us," Norman pointed out.

"Four? What about Milo?"

They all laughed. Of course, they never left the dog out of anything. At Halloween, Milo was dressed like a spider and joined Sadie and Norman in trick or treating. At Easter, he joined in the easter egg hunt – though he hunted pieces of ham. And every year on May 14th, they celebrated Milo's birthday with a dog-friendly cake and the correct number of candles.

"So, the rules," Charlie declared, taking out a piece of

paper as Janet handed the crackers out. "Festive fellows beware – for once the first cracker is pulled, the chaos will not end until the final cracker has snapped."

He pulled a face and the children laughed. "Chaos? What have they put in these crackers?"

They laughed again, mocking what was evidently a silly game.

"If, however, anyone is to lose their life – this cannot be reversed, and the festive fellows should be aware of this." He grinned at his family. "Right, so no one die from laughing at the cracker jokes."

They all chuckled again, and Charlie carried on reading.

"Each cracker has horrific consequences that all of the festive fellows must deal with. Start the game at your peril."

He shook his head and added, "This is ridiculous. Let's just do them."

Janet and Sadie picked up a cracker and went to pull it.

Then Charlie read the last line: "If you decide to stop pulling the crackers before the last one has been pulled, then death will befall you."

Death? This is going a bit far, isn't it?

Fine to make up a silly game, but to keep threatening death?

Suddenly, Charlie felt queasy. He didn't like this. It wasn't funny. He wasn't sure he wanted to share this with his family anymore.

And a bit of him – the irrational side that wouldn't let his feet hang out of the duvet at night, or walk under a ladder – worried that this might be true.

Ridiculous idea, but he decided against it.

"Wait, I think we should–"

SNAP.

Janet and Sadie pulled the first cracker.

And Charlie stared at them, dread filling his chest.

4 CRACKERS TO GO

Nothing happened.

At least, not at first.

And it seemed that the whole thing was a tad silly.

What did he expect? That something horrible would actually happen?

He was being ridiculous.

He breathed a sigh of relief.

Then he heard it.

He turned, curiously, to the dining room door. Stared at its passage as the sound grew louder, like a cross between the sound of a grasshopper, and the buzz of bees.

"What is that?" he asked.

Before anyone could reply, a swarm of locusts soared into the room and surrounded them.

He tried to bat them away, but their beady eyes and spindly legs and spotted bodies just kept circling him and circling him.

A few landed on his head and he screamed, hitting them off.

They landed on all the food, ruining any chance of a delicious Christmas dinner.

"Quick, into the living room!" Charlie instructed, and they all stood from the table and ran. He collected the crackers and brought them with him, though he wasn't sure why – instinct, perhaps. If the rules were true, they would need the rest of them.

He opened the living room door and, after they'd all made it inside, he slammed it behind them. A few locusts made it in. Charlie hit one against the wall, squished one with his foot, and noticed that his family was doing the same. Janet was hitting them away, Sadie was stomping on a few, Norman had taken a newspaper from the coffee table that he was using to splat them against the wall, and Milo was crunching one up in his mouth.

When there were no locusts left, they stood in silence, staring at each other. Dishevelled. Hair messy, clothes scruffy, panting.

"What the hell was that?" Charlie blurted out.

The others didn't respond. None of them could even venture a guess.

He glared at the crackers he'd discarded on the floor.

"They were all over the Christmas dinner," sobbed Janet. "I'd been cooking that since this morning..."

Charlie put his arms around her and kissed her forehead.

"Right," he decided. "We open no more crackers. We are done with them. Understood?"

The children nodded in agreement.

"Janet?"

She didn't reply.

"Janet, do you agree?"

Still nothing.

Then her faced turned red and she started choking. Like something was stuck down her throat.

Janet fell out of his arms and dropped to the floor, clinging to her neck. Wriggling. Writhing. Trying desperately to breathe, but somehow unable.

"Janet? Honey?"

He knelt beside her, stroking her hair back. She stared at him with a vulnerability he rarely saw in her. She never let anyone see her weaknesses, and to see her struggling was a shock.

"Janet?" he said, a little more frantically.

He put a hand on her cheek, on her throat, on her body, trying to think of what to do. She wasn't choking on anything. She was just suffocating for no reason.

"Janet!"

His eyes raised to the crackers. He hesitated, but not for long. The rules had said that if they tried to stop the game, 'death would befall them.' He knew what he had to do to save his wife.

He picked up the next cracker.

The instant he did this, she stopped choking and gasped for air.

"Honey? Are you okay?"

She rolled onto her front, then pushed herself to her knees. With her hair over her face, and her cheeks flushed, she grumbled, "Pull it."

With a sigh, and a sense of dread for what was to come, he lifted the cracker to Norman.

Normal took the other end, looked his father in the eyes, and pulled.

3 CRACKERS TO GO

A piece of paper fell out of the cracker and floated to the floor.

Charlie stared at it, and his family stared at him. He knew it was up to him to read it, but he didn't want to.

He dreaded what it said.

But he did not want his wife to start choking again so, reluctantly, he placed his thumb and forefinger around the piece of paper, lifted it to his face, and read.

"Beware the pets in your house, for they become beasts."

They frowned at each other, then turned to Milo, who had been sitting peacefully in the corner.

Except now, he wasn't sitting peacefully. And he looked nothing like the friendly dog who had once laid on a blanket beside a baby Norman when he was just a puppy; the picture of which was hanging on the wall above the fireplace. His eyes were not cute and blue, they were bloodshot and red. Saliva gathered in the corners of his mouth and his drool dripped on the floor. He showed his teeth, growling as he readied himself to pounce.

"No, not Milo," Charlie whimpered.

Milo pounced on Sadie, took her to the floor, and she screamed. She tried to cover her face, but Milo dug his teeth into her arms and drew blood.

Charlie ran to his daughter, barged his shoulder into Milo, and knocked him to the floor.

Sadie hid behind her mother, pressing her hand on her wound, blood seeping between her fingers.

"Milo, please," Charlie begged. "Don't do this."

Milo growled again and ran at Norman. Norman tried to run, but barely made it a step before Milo took him to the floor and mounted his back.

Norman wriggled but could do nothing about the rabid animal digging its teeth into his back. Norman screamed, tears glistening on his cheeks.

Charlie, once again, barged into Milo and knocked him to the floor.

He put out a calming hand as Norman joined Sadie, hiding behind their mother.

"Please, Milo. Please."

Milo growled again and leapt upon Charlie, taking him to the floor.

As Milo tried desperately to get past Charlie's arms and sink his teeth into Charlie's neck, Charlie's instincts overtook him. He had no choice.

He loved Milo, but he had to protect his family.

He shoved Milo off and tucked his arms around the dog's neck.

He squeezed.

His family stared, somewhere between terror and shock, as their family pet struggled and cried.

Charlie tried to fight away the tears as he squeezed

harder and harder. The dog struggled, so Charlie had to tighten his grip even more.

He thought of the day he picked Milo up.

Nine years and ten months ago.

Milo was weeks old. He'd spent his first day at home playing with his new toys and peeing on the carpet.

Charlie knew he was going to love this dog until the day it died. That he was going to protect it. That it would be as good as a child to him.

That dog, the one who followed Charlie from room to room as he tried to work, fell limp in his arms.

Charlie, aware that Milo might just be unconscious, continued squeezing for what felt like an eternity.

When he was ready, he dropped the carcass to the floor and turned away. He refused to look at it. He could feel his family's stares, and he could feel the tears on his cheeks, and he hated that he had ever ordered those damn crackers.

He stood. Straightened his shirt. Smoothed back his hair. And turned to his wife.

"Just pull the next one," he instructed.

2 CRACKERS TO GO

Sadie and Janet pulled the cracker, and barely a second went by before it happened. Charlie's mind didn't catch up with his eyes and, before he had acknowledged the flames that streamed out of the cracker, the room was on fire.

The furniture was alight. The coffee table was alight. The windowsills were alight. The living room where they had grown as a family was ablaze.

It seemed as if, whether by mercy or as a cruel irony, the crackers had spared the parts of the room where the family stood. They each had a small circle of carpet, separated from each other by fire; Charlie and the body of his dog on one spot, and his wife and children on others.

"Janet!" he shouted over the roars and crackles of the flames.

"Charlie! I'm here!"

"Where are the kids?"

The flames lashed back and forth. In the brief moment between lashes, Charlie caught sight of Sadie, huddling in a corner, rocking back and forth. Similarly,

Norman was stood on another spot, weeping and shaking with fear.

"Where's the next cracker? Can you see it?"

The rules said that, once all crackers were pulled, it would end. If he could just pull the next one, then the one after that, then the flames and the locusts would go.

Would he get Milo back?

Who knows?

It was hardly like he'd played this sick game before.

He just had to make it through the next challenge without losing anyone else.

"I don't know!" Janet called back. "I can't see it!"

Charlie looked around. He found it between his feet and Milo's paws.

"I got it!"

He picked it up. Went to pull it, then hesitated.

He wasn't prepared for another surprise.

"Charlie! Hurry up!"

He knew he should hurry up. He knew it needed to be done. But what would come out of the cracker next?

He pulled it, dreading the answer to that question – but it was not what would come out of the cracker that caused his terror; this time, it was what the cracker sucked into it.

1 CRACKER TO GO

Janet, Sadie and Norman flew into the air, circling each other in the smoke, and soared toward the open cracker, shrinking until they were the size of a pencil sharpener before disappearing.

"Janet?" Charlie whispers. "Sadie? Norman?"

He looked inside the cracker.

At first, he thought that they'd just been shrunk. But they weren't in there.

Dear God, where could they be?

"No..."

He fell to his knees, cherishing the cracker in his open palms. The heat faded into the background as he wept over a few bits of cardboard.

He was a grown man.

A rational man.

What the hell was going on?

Was he having a breakdown? Was he in a padded cell right now, bouncing of the walls, the hallucinations of deep-seated psychosis playing his deepest fears in front of his mind?

Or had his family actually just been sucked into a Christmas cracker?

He huffed.

He couldn't let them stay in there.

He needed resolve. Determination. Courage.

He couldn't be the pathetic morsel he was being, sat on his knees, crying over his mistakes.

He needed to pull the final damn cracker.

He stood. Placed the cracker his family were sucked into beside the body of the dog he'd killed. Looked around.

It must be in here somewhere.

He scanned the floor around his feet, hoping it would be as easy to find as the previous cracker. When he couldn't see it, he looked again. Checked his pockets. Checked beneath the dog. Scanned the floor a third time.

It wasn't there.

He turned to the rest of the room, flames separating him from wherever the cracker might be.

Then he saw it. On top of a shelf, above the fire, next to his collection of Norman Wisdom DVDs.

It was across the room, above the flames, and if he climbed onto the fireplace, he might just be able to reach it.

With a deep breath, he forced himself to be strong, told himself he could do it, willed himself to believe, and edged toward the fireplace.

The flames reached out for him, licking at his skin.

He stepped back, took a run up, and leapt, stumbling as his feet skidded off the smooth marble surface. He almost fell into the fire, but he managed to balance into a crouch.

He looked at the cracker again. Checking it was still

there. Telling himself that he was closer to it than he was a second ago.

Still crouching, and struggling to balance on such a small space, he edged to the other side of the fireplace.

He tried reaching an arm up to grab the cracker, but his fingers barely grazed it.

He was going to need to stand.

He took another deep breath, choking on the fumes. He ignored the fire that he could quite easily fall into, reminded himself he'd do anything for his family, and rose from a crouch into a hunch.

Then, using the wall to keep him steady, he stood upright, balancing precariously, and he reached for the cracker. His hand nudged the end, but it was still too far away.

He pressed a finger on the edge of the cracker and dragged it closer.

It twisted slightly, with the opposite side of the cracker hanging off the shelf, and the fire raging below.

He paused. Blinked away the sweat dripping in his eyes. Clenched his teeth. Told himself he could do this.

And he stretched his arm further.

He placed a finger on the top and dragged it closer again, but it twisted once more, until half of the cracker perched over the edge of the shelf.

One more wrong move and he'd lose it.

"Come on," he told himself. "Come on, you can do this."

He pushed down on the cracker again and dragged it closer.

It twisted.

And it dropped.

He clambered for it, trying to grab it as it left the shelf, but it escaped his grip and fell into the flames, the cardboard disintegrating into nothing within seconds.

He stared at it.

Did nothing else, just stared.

The cracker became nothing.

As did he.

And he couldn't help but scream.

It took more than an hour until the fire officers managed to contain the blaze, and longer than that until they were able to go in and check for survivors.

All they found were two bodies. One, a middle-aged man, burnt to death. Another, a dog, reduced to charred remains.

When the man's sister arrived, concerned for the welfare of her family, she asked the fire officer in charge, "Where are the rest of them?"

"The rest of who?"

"My brother's family? He has a wife and two children."

The fire officer looked confused, then turned back to his men, and demanded they go back in and do a more thorough search.

But there were no more bodies to be found.

"Maybe they weren't there?"

"That's not possible. I spoke to them on Skype – they said they weren't leaving the house."

They searched again.

Once they were sure it was safe, they even let her go in and look for herself.

Confused, she travelled around town, going to their favourite playground, favourite dog walking spots, schools, workplaces; any place she associated with her brother and his family.

Morning arrived, and they still hadn't been found.

In fact, a whole year went by, and after 365 days, the police could offer no suggestions as to what might have happened to the family.

What was found, however, by a police officer called Neil, was a curious package. Whilst the entire house was ruined, with all items blackened and charred, there was one thing that remained.

A box of crackers, sitting neatly on the dining room table.

He knew he should report this; that he should let his sergeant know. But, for a reason he could not articulate, he didn't. Instead, he put the box under his arm and took it home.

His body wouldn't be found until Boxing Day.

CHRISTMAS IN HELL

Hell is not typically a popular tourist destination. Which is a shame, as it's so full of interesting people

I suppose I can understand why people don't want to go – the spewing lava, the hot coals, and the screams of the eternally damned. But it's such a shame – as there are many things to see.

So I sat down with Satan this year to ask him what he's doing to push Hell as a Christmas getaway, and it was an illuminating chat. Here is how it went.

RICK
Hello, and thank you for joining me for this year's
Christmas anthology.

SATAN
It's a pleasure.

RICK
And how are you?

SATAN
Very well, Rick, and yourself?

RICK

Very good. So, what should I call you? I mean, you have so many names – Satan, The Devil, Lucifer, Beelzebub, Evil Incarnate...

SATAN

Satan is fine. Although, my mum sometimes calls me Satie.

RICK

Satan is fine. Now, tell me about this time of year – is it an important one for you?

SATAN

Well, yes, you see – people's happiness seems to peak at this time of year, so it makes my job a lot tougher, and a lot more important.

RICK

And how do you combat that extra happiness?

SATAN

Ah, you know, the normal – just encourage as many sins as possible. Make a man buy his mistress a more expensive gift than he gets his wife, get a boy to covet his neighbour's toys, the standard.

RICK

And do you get many new entrants?

SATAN

It doesn't increase, but we're always busy. You know, there's just so many ways for people to sin nowadays. It used to be that the rules were so stringent, but now, with people allowing lots of different beliefs in the world, there's not as many restrictions. People tend to sin quite a bit more.

RICK

And do you handle the new entrants personally?

SATAN

Not usually. I mean, for just the standard person, I will normally let Balaam, or anyone in the rest of the legion to sort it. The big names, though – I want to be there for them.

RICK

Any big names we'd know?

SATAN

Oh, of course. Osama Bin Laden, he was a big one – I had a special pit of fire prepared for him. Many of the big names we take in actually end up working for me in the end. For example, a few years ago, I allowed Jack the Ripper to surgically remove Charles Manson's insides. He was delighted, I must say.

RICK

Gosh. Right, so this interview is obviously about Christmas.

SATAN

Ah, yes, of course. I do apologise, I am very passionate
about what I do, and I tend to get side-tracked.

RICK

Not a problem. So is Christmas an important time
for you?

SATAN

Yes and no. Historically, it's been a season where people
wish to celebrate positivity and all that. But, more recently,
I've been trying to promote Hell a bit more. I don't see
why we can't share the season too.

RICK

And what are your usual Christmas plans?

SATAN

Well, unfortunately, some of us have to work on
Christmas Day – eternal torment and torture of the guilty
doesn't just end because Santa's been, you know?

RICK

Of course.

SATAN

But I do try to take an hour off, here or there, maybe to
have some turkey. It's flame grilled on the fire pits of Hell
– I tell you, there is nothing like it.

RICK

Do you enjoy Christmas dinner?

SATAN

Yes, though there isn't really anywhere in Hell that
vegetables can grow, what with the constant fire and all
that, so we have to be inventive. Last year, instead of
carrots and parsnips, I ate the intestines of a man who'd
had sex with his wife's sister. The juicier the sin, the
juicier the insides.

RICK

And I hear you're doing a lot to make Hell festive this
year?

SATAN

We are indeed. We can't necessarily get all the decorations
we require, but we make do with what we have.

RICK
Such as?

SATAN

Well, we couldn't get mistletoe, so I strung up a set of
tongues and attached a fig. We have stockings full of
children's tears. Hitler, Henry VIII and Saddam Hussain
play their annual game of Charades. And Christmas trees
are hard to come by, so I stretch out some discarded flesh
and hang ornaments off it. With the Christmas trees we
do have, we use ears instead of baubles. It really is quite
fetching, though it catches fire a lot.

RICK

And I heard you are doing a drive to encourage more
people to come?

SATAN

I am indeed – and I have attached a few promotional images we have created do give you a sense of what you can expect.

RICK

Thank you very much – I guess it would probably be best if we let our readers look at these images themselves.

SATAN

It would explain it best.

RICK

Lovely, well thank you for joining us, Satan.

SATAN

It's been a pleasure.

(Promotional images attached on following pages)

CHRISTMAS TIME IN

HELL

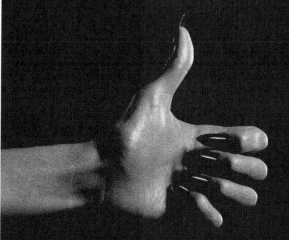

A FUN CHRISTMAS DAY OUT FOR THE WHOLE FAMILY!

SANTA VS KRAMPUS
PART THREE

The snow crumbles in his ear. It sounds like the ocean tide falling away. He lifts his head and rubs it out of his eyes, feeling pieces of snow turn to ice on his beard.

Krampus raises its head, a gleeful sneer mocking Santa's pain.

Santa turns and runs, as fast as one can run in thick snow, toward his sleigh.

Krampus's hooves follow. Slowly. Not to chase him, but to torment him. To give him hope that he will get away; hope that Krampus will snatch away at the final moment.

Santa reaches his sleigh and dives into the compartment beneath it. From there, he takes a grenade, unpins it, and looks at his enemy.

"Take this!"

He throws the grenade. Krampus leaps out of the way as it lands beside its hoofprints, the grand explosion only managing to waft the rags on the monster's back.

He has a hell a of leap, I'll give him that.

Santa takes another grenade, removes the pin, and throws it, then takes another, removes the pin, throws it, another, removes pin, throws.

Each one detonates on the ground just as Krampus leaps away – until the last one, which seems to catch it in the blast, and this time it doesn't get up.

Its body lays in the snow. Its hoof twitches. It doesn't move.

This could be a trick.

Santa knows to be cautious, even if his heart is racing in hope that he's won.

He takes a spear from beneath the sleigh, inspecting the sharp point at its tip, and trudges through the thick white.

He slows down as he nears the body.

He readies his spear, sure that Krampus will leap up at any moment and swipe its claws across Santa's throat.

Krampus doesn't move.

"Come on, you son of a bitch. I know you're still alive."

Nothing.

He edges forward again.

"I've never killed you that easily."

He reaches Krampus's side, holding the spear above his shoulder, ready to strike at any moment.

Krampus's eyes remain closed.

Maybe it is unconscious.

Santa isn't taking any risks. He takes his spear in both hands, lifts it high above his head, and plunges it down toward Krampus's heart.

Krampus catches it in its claws and snaps the spear in half.

Santa turns to run, but Krampus scrapes a claw down his back, forcing him to scream as he falls to the snow, a line of glistening red beside him.

Krampus flexes its claws around Santa's throat, lifts him up, and chuckles as he chokes.

His legs kick. His arms thrash. His heart thuds.

Splodges of light take over his vision. He is losing oxygen. He's going to pass out.

In a move he hasn't done since his youth, he swings his legs up, past his fat belly, and lands them around Krampus's arm. He tightens them against its elbow and twists, forcing Krampus to loosen his grip and allowing Santa to breathe.

Santa drops to the floor.

He looks back at his sleigh.

If he can get to that, he can speed away. Krampus will chase him, but what else is Santa supposed to do?

How are you meant to kill a creature that is so much bigger and stronger?

Fuck it. He'll figure it out in the sleigh.

He tries to run, the snow slowing him down, the blizzard bombarding his face. He's lost his hat, and somehow, this annoys him more than anything. People know him by the white beard and the red hat. Without the hat, who is he?

I'm Santa, that's who.

The reminder spurs him on.

Krampus leaps in front of him, blocking his route to the sleigh. It reaches its claw toward Santa's neck, and he grabs it, trying to push it away; but Krampus is too strong. Despite using all his strength, the claw still edges toward his face, Krampus's cocky sneer visible in his periphery.

Santa lets the claw go quite suddenly, moving to the side, forcing the claw to land deep in the snow and take Krampus off balance.

He uses the opportunity again to hurry toward his sleigh. He climbs in, flicks the reins, and Prancer and Dancer take off. The two of them still only manage to hover the sleigh off the ground, but it's enough. They may not be flying high, but they are flying quickly, and that's what matters.

Even so, he can hear the hooves of Krampus pounding the ground behind him, its pursuit creating echoes in the storm.

He flicks the reins again, urging them to go quicker. But they are already at maximum speed.

The hooves stop for a moment, and, out of the thick snowstorm, Krampus's silhouette reveals itself. Its body soars closer and lands on the sleigh behind him, causing the sleigh to buckle.

Santa lets go of the reins and turns. The reindeer will know to keep going.

He rolls up his sleeves. Readies his fists. If it comes down to this, then this is what it comes down to.

They leave the North Pole and find themselves metres over the surface of the Atlantic ocean.

This gives Santa an idea. Krampus hates water. As far as he knows, it can't swim. If he could just tilt Krampus over the edge...

The reindeer pick up speed. The air batters against his eardrums. They are going so fast that it surely won't be long until they reach land. Santa has to act quickly.

He climbs over the seat, toward the monster, and swings a fist. Krampus catches it. Squeezes it. The pressure on his fingers makes him sweat. He worries they are about to break. He swings his other fist at Krampus's chest. It surprises it enough to loosen Krampus's grip on his fist, but it would be a stretch to claim that it causes any pain.

Santa dives into Krampus's waist, trying to take barge it into the water – he only nudges it to the edge of the sleigh. But it's enough. If he could just make it topple over...

The storm lessens, then they leave it behind completely. The still of night creates clarity in Santa's mind as they move from the Atlantic Ocean to the Greenland Sea.

Santa pushes and pushes, puts all his might into forcing Krampus to the edge, determined to send it into the water and be free of it.

Krampus doesn't budge. It just smirks and laughs. Mocking the fat old man's feeble attempt at strength.

Krampus shoves Santa off and raises up, balancing on the edge of the sleigh.

In the distance, Santa sees mountains. They are approaching Svalbard, and the tiny Norwegian mountains Santa normally sails over at the beginning of his Christmas Eve journey.

Santa tries to shove Krampus over the side again, but Krampus merely pushes him off.

Then Krampus raises his claw. Readies the death swipe.

And, just as Krampus is about to end this battle, the sleigh passes the odd looks of a few polar bears and collides with the snowy mountains of Nordaustlandet.

Santa is thrown from the sleigh, unaware where the reindeer or his sled or Krampus go, just rolling down the mountain, picking up speed, feeling a sharp sting each time he collides with the ground. The snow isn't as thick as in the North Pole; he can feel the rocks beneath it.

After tumbling for enough time to create agony across Santa's entire body, he collides with something – a tree, or a rock, or a pylon; he's not sure – and he stops falling.

He rolls over, groaning, feeling every part of his ageing body betray him.

And he hears the hooves of Krampus in the distance.

Santa Vs Krampus concludes later in the anthology.

ANOTHER LETTER FROM SIMON

Dear Santa,

Well, I must really say that, for the second year running, you quite outdid yourself.

I was delighted last Christmas, having crafted a list of items I imagined you might find unreasonable, to discover my Christmas tree adorned with the most fanciful of gifts.

I unwrapped a squidgy package with the intestines of a good woman, whilst opening a separate box to find an elf, dressed in a tutu, shackled to a pole. I mean, really, I was barely expecting one thing from my list – and you provided two! What a wonderful surprise.

As I do not wish to make you complacent, this year's list is going to be a tad more ambitious. You have fulfilled my requirements quite sufficiently over the last two years, so let's see if you are able to do so again this year.

Oh, and Santa, please try to be even more discreet if you can. Last year, there was only one woman tied up in my basement that I did not wish you to wake up. This year, however, there are fifteen. Although there may be fewer by the time you get here. I am feeling rather hungry, and I'm due to have guests.

Oh, and whilst I have you, if you feel like plunging my toilets whilst you're here, please do go ahead. It may sound like an odd request, but all those fingers and toes keep blocking my drains. There are only so many plumbers I can call out until people start to get suspicious as to why these plumbers keep disappearing.

And I don't really like plumbers, they are usually quite chewy – something to do with all the filth, I think.

Anyway, I digress.

Here is my list:

Two turtle doves. I'm really intrigued to see what the offspring of a turtle and a dove actually looks like.

That girl from Twilight. I'd like to see if removing her spleen will give her a bit of personality.

A ticket to Disneyland. Mickey Mouse and I have a long-standing feud that needs to be put to an end, once and for all.

A set of identical twins and some really strong superglue. I think you know what I want to do.

Any white middle-class man who claims that anti-racism messages are taking their rights away. Let's be honest, they need to die.

Enough peanut butter to cover the entire body of an adult male, and a dog who enjoys licking. I trust there will be no further questions asked.

Anyone who has ever been on Jerry Springer.

Matter of fact, give me Jerry Springer too. I love his final thought segment of the show, and I'd like to see what his final, final thought would be.

Anyone who goes into schools and preaches abstinence to teenagers, and a bed that can withstand a lot of vigorous movement. I'm willing to show them why they are wrong.

Grown adults who play World of Warcraft.

Also, some deodorant for those grown adults who play World of Warcraft. I don't want that smell in my house.

A feminist and a mansplainer, locked together in a room for eternity. I want to see who kills the other one first.

Adele's ex-boyfriend. I've often wondered what was so bad about him.

A reindeer, a whip, some lubricant, and five hours in a sleazy motel room. An explanation is not necessary.

The kid from *The Snowman*, but as an adult trying to convince the doctors that he really did see a snowman come to life.

The phone number for the demon who possessed Emily Rose. We should hang out.

Three elves and three stripper poles.

Failing this, three elves and one stripper pole.

In fact, forget the pole. The elves should be able to perform without.

Theresa May and a field of wheat. I like watching a woman be naughty.

A picture of Mrs Claus eating a whole carrot. Or a parsnip. Or a banana. In fact, let's go with the banana.

Also, I'd like to have that banana.

The head of anyone who likes mushy peas. What's wrong with you?

The heart of anyone called Jonathan who refers to themselves as Jonno. No one likes that guy.

A video of Megan Fox trying to push out a really stubborn poo. I need to see something that makes her look less appealing, as right now she's so hot it's just ridiculous.

A copy of *Woman Scorned*. I don't know if I mentioned it, but that Rick Wood is a wonderful author. And he's a good-looking chap, too. And friendly. Helpful. Gives to charity. And, what's more, he's incredibly modest.

Also, I saw a man on the news who claimed that "foreigners keep coming over, stealing our jobs, then they don't even work." I would like him impaled on a javelin. Not just for me, but for the sake of the world.

And, finally, a partridge in a pear tree.

(By partridge, I mean hooker. By pear tree, I mean the guts of that hooker.)

All the best, Santa, and a very merry Christmas.

    Yours,

    Simon.

    (The Christmas Cannibal.)

'TWAS THE NIGHT BEFORE MURDER PART 3

(Parts 1 & 2 in Volumes 1 & 2)

'Twas the night before Christmas and Kris Kringle was gone,
It had been a whole year since things had gone wrong,
After shooting up the grotto he lives in a cell,
And poor Mrs Claus has been going through hell,
Now her husband's in the clink, she runs the show,
She had no idea how bad it could go,
She'd seen Father Claus do it, and he'd done his best,
But she was starting to get weighed down by the stress.

Every day she fed reindeer and organised elves,
Went through naughty and nice lists she kept on the shelves,
Tried to make it round the world in just one night,
And tried to do all this whilst doing it right,
Eventually one day an elf posed a question,

He thought things could be better and he had a suggestion,
Oh, that poor elf, he was down on his luck,
She shoved a candy cane in his heart and shouted, "Get fucked!"

She shattered her mirror and was covered in cuts,
Now she finally knew why her husband went nuts,
After having to deal with another elf's voice,
In their stupid falsetto (which wasn't their choice,)
She decided she couldn't take it anymore,
So she burst into the grotto with an almighty roar,
With her eyes almost bursting and the moon up high,
She said with a laugh, "You're all gonna die!"

An elf cried out, "It's happened again, she's lost her head!"
Then another cried out – well, nothing, they were dead,
She'd impaled him with a little toy car,
Shoved a Barbie up his arse and shoved it quite far,
Tied tinsel round his throat and squeezed, it was awful,
Then threw down the tree and smashed every bauble,
The elves, the poor chaps, could do nothing but flee,
As she boomed out over them, "You can't get away from me!"

She put a virus on the admin computer,
Then blew up the control room with a massive bazooka,
Smeared the elves' hats with loads of nits,
Then laced the elves' food with laxatives,
She found all the elves whilst they were deep in focus,
And opened the cage to a load of pet locusts,
Then fed a few elves to some elf cannibals,
And once she was done, she turned to the animals.

She burst into the barn with two mighty blows,
Grabbed Rudolph's head and laughed at his nose,
"Everyone loves how it's red, well that won't last,"
And she sat on his face, and it went up her arse,
She giggled and giggled like it was something light-
hearted,
And he tried to struggle as she farted and farted,
Once she let him go, she laughed with a sneer,
And now he is known as the brown-nosed reindeer.

She set out on the sleigh when it was time to leave,
Put on the Santa suit and brushed off the sleeves,
With the grotto in flames, she crossed over the ocean,
Making her plans with the sleigh's every motion,
She started in Germany as she cackled with glee,
And broke into the home of her first family,
Pinned down a woman as her man cried "don't hurt her,"
And choked her to death with a stale frankfurter.

Later, whilst in France, she beat up a dad,
Tied up his family and grabbed his gonad,
Oh, how his knees shook, he started to cower,
As she used a cheese knife to slice his Eiffel tower,
She said to herself, "Well this is just fine,"
Then dropped in on the family of the country's top mime,
As she burst in and unleashed all kinds of violence,
She found it bizarre how they all screamed in silence.

Next, she crossed the shore and entered the states,
Dropped in on the Trumps as if they were mates,
She beat him up bad, and the fat lump did lose,
Still the next day he claimed it was fake news,
She locked him in the basement and he was aggrieved,

She built a wall around it so he couldn't leave,
As she flew away, she called out, "See you later!"
After using his manifesto to replace his toilet paper.

By the time she was done, the world was in tatters,
But she didn't really think any of it matters,
She'd had her fun, now the cops did give chase,
Oh, how she despised the whole human race,
She tried to leave the country, but they caught her the
next day,
They put her in the cell and threw the keys away,
But don't feel sad for her, don't ever fear,
At least she'll spend Christmas with her husband this
year.

CHRISTMAS NIGHT OF THE LIVING DEAD: YEAR TWO

1

T he house had been fixed in darkness since Boxing Day the previous year, and Chet had lived in it for 363 days.

It was surprising how little time society had taken to crumble. At first, they thought it was a pandemic. Then the dead got up and started walking, and no one knows of a virus that can make them do that.

By the time they had gobbled down the last few mouthfuls of their Christmas Day feast, the government had fallen. By the time they'd argued over a game of charades, half of the world's population had turned. By the time the end credits of whatever generic Santa Claus movie they'd fallen asleep watching had rolled, society had ended, and there was a knock on the door.

Chet had woken, slightly perturbed, and looked to his mum and dad. They were still fast asleep. As was his sister and her husband.

Then the knock came again.

Who on earth knocks on a door on Christmas Day night?

Chet considered waking his family, but he didn't. He'd just turned eighteen. He was an adult now, just like them. He could deal with it himself.

He'd pushed himself up and rubbed his eyes as the knock resounded through the house again. It was so loud, he wasn't quite sure how the others hadn't woken up. He trudged through the hallway and unlocked the door.

He opened it.

Within an hour, his sister and her husband were dead.

Within two hours, he'd had to kill them.

His parents had told him to run while they stayed and fought. He wished he could say that he'd protested, or that he'd stayed and helped his parents. But he can't. He ran like hell.

When he came back on Boxing Day, there was nothing left. Nothing living or unliving, that is. There were plenty of guts and limbs and blood, but the home was otherwise empty.

And now, a year on, he thought back to that day, just like he had every other day, and he let the guilt fester. It was particularly strong today, what with it approaching the anniversary of his cowardly act. Sometimes, when he relived the day in his mind, he changed events. He would let his daydreams play out a scenario where he stayed, or where his sister hadn't died, or where he hadn't opened the damn door in the first place.

Then the daydream would end, and nothing would have changed.

"Chet!"

"Coming."

He pushed himself up from the corner of the room. Sighed. Brushed dust from the floorboards off his trousers. Not that it made much difference, they were still filthy – he could hardly pop out to Gap to get another pair.

He took his candle and used it as his guide out of the room and through the hallway. Strong, sturdy planks of wood covered the windows. He hadn't seen daylight in months.

He entered the kitchen and the sight almost made him cry. Jeanie, Harry and Cal all sat at the table, an inadequate but much appreciated Christmas feast in front of them.

Jeanie had been insistent that they would have a Christmas meal; that they would attempt some normality in what was a very abnormal situation. She'd found a live turkey whilst scavenging for food a few months ago and had kept it in the study, ready to eat today. There was plenty of meat. The vegetables, however, were lacking – there were a few carrots from tins they'd kept, along with peas and chickpeas. They'd been saving a bottle of wine they'd found months ago, and they each had a glass.

"This is amazing," Chet said.

Jeanie beamed. She'd done her best.

"Dig in," she said, chopping up her turkey.

Chet looked around at his new family. They were all friends he'd known from school, albeit not friends he associated with in the corridors of St. Patrick's High. Jeanie was an advocate of math's club, Harry was captain of the rugby team, and Cal used to paint his nails black. What an eclectic mix they were.

He wouldn't change it for anything.

In a moment of inspiration, Chet lifted his glass.

"I would like to propose a toast," he said. "To the founder of the feast, Jeanie."

"Here, here," said the others, raising their glasses.

"And to friends, old and new."

"To friends, old and new," they echoed.

They all drank, and dug back into their food. Chet didn't. Not yet. Instead, he watched his friends. They were locked inside this house with no way out – the windows and doors were boarded up, and they had enough food to keep them going in this situation for months, at least. But he wasn't sad about it. He was where he belonged.

No one returned his smile. They were all too eager to devour the turkey, shovelling mouthfuls of bird into their mouth.

Chet cut a piece of turkey and looked at it. Such a small pleasure, but one that brings great joy to those that don't have much. He lifted it to this mouth.

Then he paused.

And he looked at it.

It smelt funny.

He sniffed it. It smelt like rotting flesh. Or faeces.

Maybe Jeanie hadn't managed to keep it that fresh. Maybe they were so used to tinned food that they didn't know what a juicy piece of meat smelt like anymore.

No, that was not it.

It was a strange smell.

He looked at his friends, filling their eager gobs with turkey.

They didn't seem to notice the smell.

Then he looked to the remnants of the turkey that sat on the kitchen side. A flickering candle illuminated what was left of it, and he couldn't help staring.

Something intrigued him.

He rose from his seat. Drifted across the kitchen until he stood over the turkey.

"Hey, Chet, you all right?" asked Harry.

Chet ignored him.

He pushed the candle closer to the turkey remnants. About a third of the meat was still on the bones.

He lifted the turkey up.

And he saw it.

On the underside of what used to be the turkey's belly.

Teeth marks. The size of a human jaw.

What would have bitten a turkey?

He looked around at his friends, who paused eating to stare back at him, their plates of turkey almost empty.

"Shit," he said.

2

Chet reached into the kitchen drawer and took out the sharpest knife he could find.

"Chet?"

He looked at the boarded-up windows and wondered how long it would take to find something that would pull out the many, many nails that had kept them safe.

"Chet, what are you doing?"

His eyes wandered to the door that led to the hallway, that led to the front door, and thought of the numerous bolts that kept it shut. Would he be able to find a bolt cutter somewhere in the house? And how long would it take him to break them?

"Chet, what's with the knife, dude?"

His thoughts turned to hiding places. Where could he go? He could lock the bathroom door, but it wouldn't withstand the strength of three of them for long. There was the cupboard, but zombies generally have a good sense of smell and, once they'd found him, he'd be cornered.

Jeanie rose to her feet. "Chet, why don't you tell us–"

"Stay back!"

Chet pointed the blade toward her. She put her hands in the air, but her face did not betray her confusion.

"Chet, what are you doing?"

He looked from Jeanie's concern to the puzzlement of Harry's expression, to the fear on Cal's.

"Do not come any closer!"

"Chet, what the hell are you doing?"

At first, he wondered how long it will take. The turkey was inside of them now. How long until it was in their blood stream? How long until it killed them? How long until they rose again?

Would they even die before they turned, considering it was already inside of them?

Then he thought of these people not as the undead, but as his friends. As three people who took him in when they didn't need to. All of them had lost their family, but had found a new family in each other. They hadn't been apart since New Year's Day.

And he was supposed to just accept that he was on his own again?

He was supposed to come to terms with these people loving him one moment, then trying to eat him the next?

"Chet, put down the fucking knife, you're scaring us."

He stared into Jeanie's eyes. Maybe they would turn first. They weren't bloodshot, or fully dilated, or even red – but he expected the change any moment, and he waited for a sign.

"Chet, why don't you–"

"The turkey!" he blurted out. "You've all eaten the turkey!"

Jeanie glanced at the others, each sharing a look of perplexity.

"We all have, yes."

"I haven't!"

"Then why don't you sit down and have some?"

"You don't understand!"

"No, I don't, but if you just explain–"

"Look!"

Chet grabbed the turkey and lifted it up by the leg bones. Beside the candle, the bite mark is clear. They all stare at it, and no one makes a sound.

Their glances at each other are no longer confused, but terrified. They look at what little turkey is left on their plate. Drop their cutlery. Stand up and back away from the table. As if getting distance from the remains of their food will make a difference.

"But I checked it..." Jeanie said. "I checked it..."

"Did you check the belly?"

Jeanie went to reply, then her eyes widened.

"We need to be sick," she decided. "We all need to throw it up, right now, if we–"

Too late. Her body lurched. A tuneless rasp croaked out of her mouth.

The others followed. Gargling and spitting and jerking.

"We need to get out!" Jeanie cried between convulsions. "We need to get out, so we don't hurt Chet–"

She fell to her knees. She didn't have time to leave. She spewed a mouthful of blood over the kitchen floor.

Chet suddenly realised that he'd put the door to the hallway between them and him. He had a knife, but it would do little against three of them.

Harry and Cal writhed and wriggled on the floor.

Their limbs shot in obscure directions, their necks twisting their heads from side to side, and their eyes widening.

And then their eyes changed.

And his friends were no longer alive.

Chet leapt over Jeanie's body as it squirmed and wriggled and twisted and contorted, and was just about to reach the doorway when something grabbed his ankle.

He fell to the ground and looked over to find the pale, blood-eyed, dead face of Jeanie staring at him, ravenous for meat, starving for his flesh.

He tried to wriggle free, both of them on the floor, but her grip was too tight.

Groans came from the other side of the table. Harry and Cal stood, slowly, readjusting to their new state of permanent hunger.

They looked around. Their bloodshot pupils moving from one side to the other.

Then they turned and locked their gaze on Chet.

With a scream, Chet swung the knife down onto Jeanie's wrist.

She didn't loosen her grip. It's hardly like it would cause her pain. She wouldn't feel anything now that she's dead.

Harry and Cal, knocking against each other, began their slow meander around the table.

Chet dug the knife in harder, and harder still, blood squelching out of her skin beside the blade, pouring over her cheap tattoos.

Harry and Cal hobbled around the side of the table, their arms outstretched for food.

Chet dug the knife in as hard as it would go, taking it straight through the limb, and tore through it. Jeanie's hand became loose from of the rest of her arm, and he was able to scarper away with her fingers still wrapped around his ankle, but her hand now separated from the body.

He made it to the stairs. He figured it would take them longer to understand stairs. Or maybe it wouldn't. Who knew?

He leapt up them two at a time until Jeanie's hand tripped him up. He reached down and prised apart her fingers, throwing the hand down the stairs and hitting Cal in the face, knocking him back.

Without looking to see if they were keeping up with him, he sprinted across the hallway and into the bedroom. A pile of rope stopped him from shutting the door, so he kicked it across the room, then shut himself inside.

He leant against the wall. Panting. Sweating.

Seconds later, groans approached, and there was scuffling against the door.

But they didn't know how to turn a door handle.

Which meant he was safe, for now.

He fell to his knees and breathed a huge sigh of relief.

As the terror flooded out of him, it was replaced with reality.

He couldn't stay in this room forever. There was no food. No water. He'd starve long before they did.

But even so, how was he meant to kill them?

They were his friends.

Sure, they weren't technically his friends anymore, on the account that they were no longer alive.

But they still had the same faces, albeit a little uglier. The same bodies, albeit slower. The same need to feed, albeit their diet had changed.

Even if he could face them off and win, he didn't know how he could bring himself to shove that knife into their brain.

He looked around the room for an answer, as if it was just going to leap out at him.

Then, funnily enough, it did.

The rope that had blocked the door. It was a long rope. He could cut through it and make three pieces of rope long enough to...

He turned his head toward the groans outside the door.

Maybe he didn't have to kill them after all.

C het sunk the knife into the flesh and carved through the meat, juices squeezing onto the tray below. Then he placed the pieces of turkey onto three plates and carried them to the table.

"Happy Boxing Day," he said as he placed the first plate in front of Jeanie. Her mouth snapped at his arm.

"Ah, ah, ah!" he said, thankful that the rope around her chest was keeping her in place. "None of that, thank you."

He placed the other plate in front of a bound Harry, and a bound Cal.

He took his place in front of a bowl of tinned carrots and tinned beef stew.

"Well, dig in!" he said, grinning at the others.

They all stretched their necks toward him, their teeth chattering together, their jaws snapping at his neck.

"If you don't eat your turkey, it will go cold."

They didn't seem interested in the turkey.

Ah well, maybe now would be the best time to propose the toast.

He lifted his wine glass.

"I would like to raise a glass to friends, old and new," he said. "Here's to you guys."

He drank.

The others kept snapping their jaws.

How very rude.

"Come on guys, if you don't eat it now, you'll be having it for breakfast."

He placed a mouthful of beef stew into his mouth. It was nice.

Well, compared to what he was used to eating, it was nice.

He looked around at his friends. The eager, decaying face of Jeanie, the stinking, rabid face of Harry, and the snarling, maggot ridden face of Cal.

And he smiled.

He was with his family now.

SANTA VS KRAMPUS
PART FOUR

Below the snowy mountains of Svalbard, a few rows of houses sit peacefully beside the ocean. They are quaint houses, some red, some light green, and some yellow. This may sound like an odd row of houses – but it isn't. Each one is beautiful, beside a garden of snow. Like a painting of the perfect Christmas story.

Those houses rattle as the mountains quake under the thudding of Krampus's hooves.

Santa, stuck halfway down the mountain against an electricity pylon, searches for where the sound is coming from. His sleigh is across from him, on its side. Prancer and Dancer are nowhere to be found, which is probably Santa's fault for picking the two most cowardly reindeers.

He pushes himself to his knees, then falls back to the ground. His spine throbs. His back aches. The slash down his back stings. Every limb is shaking under the pressure of pain.

But he has to keep going. He has to.

He looks to the houses at the base of the hill. They will be expecting presents in roughly twenty-four hours from now. At this rate, he won't make it until sunrise.

The ground shakes under Krampus's steps again. It's

close. Santa doesn't have much time. He will just have to deal with the pain.

He pushes himself to his knees. He doesn't try to stand. Not yet, at least. Instead, he crawls through the snow. It isn't as deep or thick as the North Pole snow. This time, however, it isn't the storm holding him back; it's his tender body.

"Come on," he urges himself. "Come on, you fat bastard – you can do this."

He drags himself forward, stretching arms, his muscles twinging, his eyes set on the sleigh.

It must only be a few steps away, yet every inch feels like ten yards.

The booms of Krampus's footsteps echo. They are louder than they were a moment ago. Much louder.

He drags himself forward, willing himself to move, to find the strength. He knows what he needs to do. He knows how to win this. He just has to find the energy. Find the resolve. Push himself, like it's the last hour of delivering presents on Christmas Eve, when he's exhausted and bloated from many mince pies – he's survived a few millennia, he can damn well survive this!

With a growl he pushes himself up, falls again, then pushes himself up once more, holding his arms out to steady himself.

He lifts one foot, ignoring the pull of his muscle and places it down.

That's one step. Just another few to go.

The ground shakes harder, snow crumbles down the slope, and a shadow looms over Santa.

He doesn't look back. He knows what's there.

He takes another step. Then another. Then another.

The shadow grows. Heavy footsteps approach.

He is almost within reach of the sleigh. He stretches his arm, and he can just about reach it; his hand grazes the side just as a claw digs into his calf.

He falls to the ground and cries out.

Then he ignores it. And he pulls himself up by his arms and throws himself over the side of the sleigh, leaving him lying on the seat.

The ugly face of Krampus appears over him. It twists to the side, looking at him like a scientist might look at a lab rat.

Santa leans all his weight to the side of the sleigh and, being as fat as he is, manages to level it. It begins to move, back down the slope, edging forward as it begins to pick up a little speed.

"Come and get me you ugly fuck."

The sleigh quickly accelerates, gravity doing the work. Santa just lays there, letting it get quicker and quicker, watching the night sky drift by, the stars shining upon him.

Krampus's hooves land on the sleigh, either side of Santa.

The sleigh picks up even more speed. They are shooting down the slope, faster and faster, wind attacking his ears.

Krampus places a claw at the side of Santa's throat, like he's finding the right place to aim at.

Santa doesn't move. He doesn't need to. He just needs to wait.

Krampus lifts its claw, about to strike, and its face contorts into a twist of anger, ready to finally rid the world of this chubby, happy charlatan.

Santa closes his eyes, waiting for the impact.

And then it hits.

Not Krampus – the sleigh. Into the side of the nearest house. Santa and Krampus are both sent flying from it, soaring through the air at a speed created by the momentum of the slope.

Santa watches as the houses and ground disappear beneath him, and the ocean becomes visible.

The sleigh flies over him, and over Krampus, and lands in the ocean with a splash, as does Santa.

Krampus, however, doesn't simply land with a splash – he is far too big and heavy for that. He lands with a thud that sends a wave of water over the small town, then sinks further and further into the sea.

Santa focusses on himself first. He thrashes his arms to stop him sinking deeper into the water, and searches for the moonlight. He moves his arms, adrenaline providing him with the little energy he has left, and takes in a big breath as he makes it to the surface.

He sees the sleigh, bobbing on the water. And he sees Krampus, thrashing about, trying desperately to stay afloat. But he can't. He's sinking and he's drowning.

Santa swims to the sleigh, trying not to get caught in the thrashes of water created by Krampus's claws. He reaches his arm onto the runner, pulls himself up the side of the sleigh, and throws himself over.

Krampus tries to thrash toward the sleigh, but it can't. It's panicking too much.

And, as Krampus becomes weaker, and the sleigh floats toward it, Santa reaches out and places a hand on the back of its weak head.

He pushes its head under the water, and holds it there until the bubbles stop.

Then its body floats to the surface, where it stays, still and empty.

Santa lays on his back. He notices that the sun is coming up. He can also hear something in the distance. Cheering.

He sits up.

There are people. The residents of Svalbard, having come out of their homes, applauding, showing their appreciation for Santa's heroic efforts.

A man drives a speedboat toward him.

Santa just lays back down and stares at the sky as the sun rises. He allows the man to attach a rope to his sleigh and drag it inland without acknowledging them. He is too tired, and in too much pain to move. He'll rest until he reaches the shore.

When he arrives back on land, a doctor is ready to see him. He gives Santa painkillers, patches up his wounds and, by the time the sun has fully risen, Santa is alert enough to know he needs to get back.

It is now Christmas Eve, and he has a job to do.

A man with a plane says he'll get it ready. A group of men retrieve the sleigh and attach it to the base of the plane with rope. Santa thanks them, and they say it's the least they could do. Once ready, the residents cheer him as he waves from the cockpit of a Cessna 172.

Meanwhile, in the middle of the Arctic Ocean, the body of a hideous creature drifts away. The residents sailed out to sea to find its carcass, but they couldn't. Of course they couldn't.

It wouldn't let them.

It is a creature of myth, more so than Santa, and how could the world live in fear if they knew whether it was alive?

And, as still as its body looks, and as vacant as its eyes are, there is still a mind in there. A despicable mind, yes, but a mind nonetheless.

And the mind did not die.

And, as its claw twitches, the body starts to live, too.

For this is a creature that won't simply drown.

It is not a creature of this world.

And it is not a creature who will give up.

Yes, Santa will have this year. Another Christmas where he'll get to make all rich kids happy and poor kids grateful.

Another Christmas to get fat on mince pies and biscuits and sherry.

But only this Christmas.

Because, as the rest of the claws twitch again, and the eyes slowly come back to life, it knows it is not defeated, just simply consumed by even more rage.

And it will be back.

As much as Christmas will come and go this year, you can be sure that Krampus will do his best again next year.

And maybe that time, he will not fail.

Maybe next year, Krampus will defeat its enemy, once and for all, and the presents you ask for to satisfy your greed will no longer arrive.

I guess you'll know when you wake up on Christmas morning, put on your Christmas socks, and rush down-stairs to find either a stocking full of presents, and toys and gifts under the tree – or a stocking full of a jolly, fat man's guts, and a Christmas tree decorated in his blood.

Perhaps, on Christmas morning, when you rush out of bed with nothing but presents on your mind, you should proceed with caution.

Perhaps, when you tiptoe downstairs and check to see if he's been, you should keep that living room door shut.

You never know what you might find.

JOIN RICK WOOD'S READER'S GROUP...

And get his horror anthology **Roses Are Red So Is Your Blood** for free!

Join at **www.rickwoodwriter.com/sign-up**

ALSO AVAILABLE BY RICK WOOD

BLOOD SPLATTER BOOKS

18+

This Book Is Full of BODIES

RICK WOOD

BLOOD SPLATTER BOOKS

18+

PSYCHO
B*TCHES

RICK WOOD

BOOK ONE IN THE SENSITIVES SERIES

THE
SENSITIVES

RICK WOOD

SHUTTER HOUSE

RICK WOOD

HOME INVASION

RICK WOOD

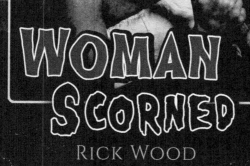

BLOOD SPLATTER BOOKS

18+

WOMAN
SCORNED

RICK WOOD

Printed in Great Britain
by Amazon

31669796R00088